# MUSEUM
# MYSTERIES

Museum Mysteries is published by Stone Arch Books
A Capstone Imprint
1710 Roe Crest Drive
North Mankato, MN 56003
www.mycapstone.com

Text and illustrations © 2016 Stone Arch Books

Library of Congress Cataloging-in-Publication Data
Brezenoff, Steven, author. The case of the stolen space suit / by Steve Brezenoff; illustrated by Lisa K. Weber.
        pages cm. -- (Museum mysteries)

Summary: When the space suit of famous astronaut Sally Ride disappears from a traveling exhibit, Amal Farah, daughter of the Air and Space Museum's archivist, and her three friends are determined to find the culprit before the exhibit is cancelled.

ISBN 978-1-4965-2516-1 (library hardcover) -- ISBN 978-1-4965-2520-8 (pbk.)
ISBN 978-1-4965-2524-6 (ebook pdf)

1. Spacesuits--Juvenile fiction. 2. Astronautical museums--Juvenile fiction.
3. Theft from museums--Juvenile fiction. 4. Criminal investigation--Juvenile fiction.
5. Detective and mystery stories. 6. Best friends--Juvenile fiction. [1. Mystery and detective stories. 2. Space suits--Fiction. 3. Astronautical museums--Fiction.
4. Museums--Fiction. 5. Stealing--Fiction. 6. Criminal investigation--Fiction. 7. Best friends--Fiction. 8. Friendship--Fiction. 9. Middle Eastern Americans--Fiction.]
I. Weber, Lisa K., illustrator. II. Title. III. Series: Brezenoff, Steven. Museum mysteries.
PZ7.B7576Cat 2016
813.6--dc23
[Fic]                                                      2015020985

Designer: K. Carlson
Editor: A. Deering
Production Specialist: K. McColley

Photo Credits: Shutterstock (vector images, backgrounds, paper textures)

Printed in China.
092015   007503LEOS16

# The Case of the
# STOLEN SPACE SUIT

By Steve Brezenoff
Illustrated by Lisa K. Weber

STONE ARCH BOOKS
a capstone imprint

# Sally Ride

- Sally Ride was born May 26, 1951, in California and attended Stanford University, where she studied physics.

- In 1977, NASA began looking for female astronauts. Sally Ride was one of six women chosen for the job.

- In 1983, Sally Ride became the first American woman to fly in space as an astronaut on a shuttle mission. Her job was to work the robotic arm to help put satellites into space.

- After leaving NASA, Sally Ride became a teacher. She came up with the idea for NASA's EarthKAM project, which lets students take pictures of Earth using a camera on the International Space Station.

- In 2003, Sally Ride was added to the Astronaut Hall of Fame.

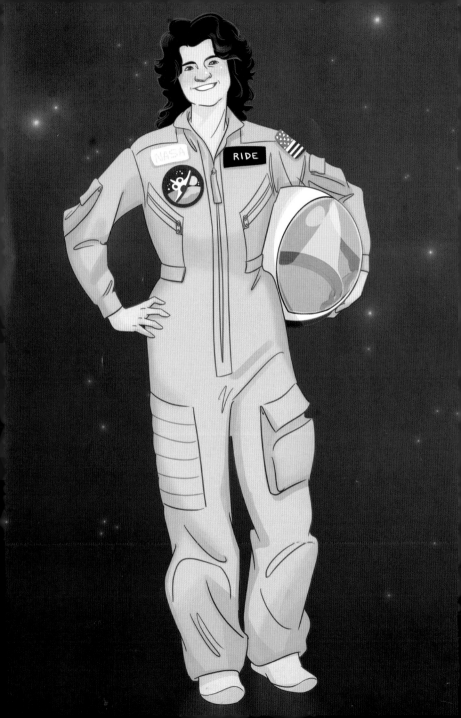

Amal Farah

Raining Sam

Wilson Kipper

Clementine Wim

# Capitol City Sleuths

### Amal Farah
Age: 11
Favorite Museum: Air and Space Museum
Interests: astronomy, space travel, and
building models of spaceships

### Raining Sam
Age: 12
Favorite Museum: American History Museum
Interests: Ojibwe history, culture, and
traditions, American history — good and bad

### Clementine Wim
Age: 13
Favorite Museum: Art Museum
Interests: painting, sculpting with clay, and
anything colorful

### Wilson Kipper
Age: 10
Favorite Museum: Natural History Museum
Interests: dinosaurs (especially pterosaurs
and herbivores) and building dinosaur models

# TABLE OF

# CONTENTS

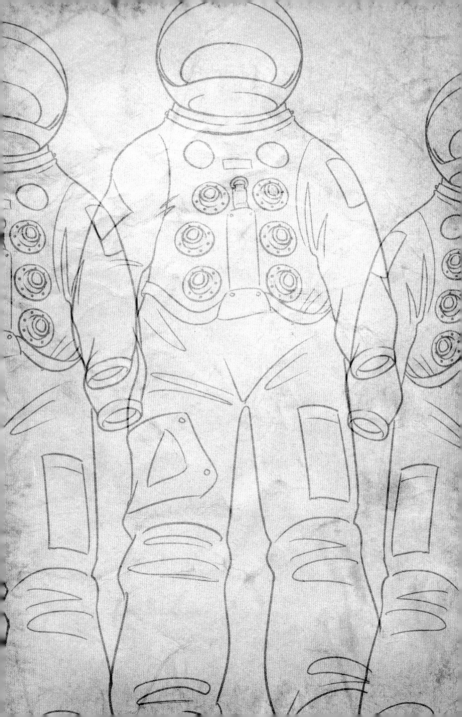

## CHAPTER 1
## Not So Boring Night

It was Friday night, and Amal Farah lay on the couch in her father's office at the Capitol City Air and Space Museum. Her history textbook sat on the floor beside the couch. She had a three-day weekend ahead of her, but she was bored and had decided she might as well get her homework out of the way now.

"Dad," Amal said without picking her head up from her pillow, "when are we *leaving*?" She didn't like to whine, but

11

sometimes it was necessary. And now was definitely one of those times. She'd been sitting in her father's office since four o'clock, right after school.

"What?" her father, Dr. Ahmed Farah, the museum's head archivist, replied. His attention was on his computer screen, not on his daughter — nor on the time.

"You said you had to stay a little late," Amal reminded him as she checked the time on her phone, "but it's almost eight o'clock. I've finished all my homework. I've texted all my friends. I've played ten levels of Fruit Basher on my phone. And on top of all that, I'm *starving*. When are we going *home*?"

Dr. Farah sighed and pulled off his reading glasses. With his thumb and index finger, he rubbed the bridge of his nose. "I'm sorry, sweetheart. There's just a lot going on. I've been butting heads with Mr. Mordecai in the Special Collections Division. He's been just furious about . . ." Dr. Farah stopped himself. "Well, it doesn't matter. We'll settle this soon, I think. Give me twenty more minutes."

Amal slid off the couch and onto the floor. "Fine," she said, picking up her history textbook. "I'll just do my homework again."

"Great idea," her father said with a smile.

Suddenly there was a loud *CRASH!* It shook the office walls and echoed through the open door.

"What was that?" Amal asked, sitting up straight.

Dr. Farah took off his glasses again and stood up. "I'm not sure. I thought we were the only ones left in the museum besides the security team."

"Let's go check it out!" Amal exclaimed, jumping to her feet.

"I'm sure security will investigate," Dr. Farah said.

But Amal grabbed her father's hand and pulled him through the office door. "It'll just take a minute," she insisted. "Let's face it. It'll be the most exciting thing that's happened to either of us since I got here."

Dr. Farah smiled a little. "Perhaps you're right," he said.

Amal led the way down the back hall of the museum. This part of the museum was off-limits to visitors, but Amal and her best friends — Wilson Kipper, Clementine Wim, and Raining Sam — had free run of the place most of the time since their parents all worked in the Capitol City network of museums.

"I don't hear anything anymore," her father said. "No point in looking around if we can't follow the noi—"

*BANG!*

*CLANG!*

*CRASH!*

"That noisy enough for you, Dad?" Amal asked. She darted around the corner and down the next hallway, leaving her father behind.

Up ahead, the lights flickered. There were eerie sounds and startling shadows around every turn. But Amal wasn't scared. She ran on, following the banging and clanging, which grew louder with every step she took.

"This way, Dad!" Amal called back over her shoulder. She didn't slow down or look behind her, and soon she reached the deepest, darkest hallway, past all the offices, beyond even the bleakest storage rooms of the maintenance department.

Amal stopped. It was a dead end. She faced a blank wall. There were no doors, no signs, and no evidence that anything existed beyond it. And yet the clanging and banging continued, ringing louder than ever from the other side of the wall.

"But there's no door here," Amal muttered to herself. She could hardly hear herself think over the noise. "There's no more museum. How can anything be making noise on the other side of this wall?"

After a moment, the noise stopped, though the clanging echoed in Amal's ears like a ringing fire alarm. Soon she heard her father's running footsteps approaching.

"Amal!" Dr. Farah called as he rounded the last corner. "Please don't run off like that again."

"Dad," Amal said, ignoring his reprimand, "the banging was coming from the other side of this wall. It doesn't make any sense."

"Why not?" Dr. Farah asked.

Amal pulled her phone from her back pocket and quickly brought up the museum's website. She clicked through to the map and found where they were. "Because there's no more museum on the other side of this wall," she said, showing him the map. "It ends here."

"I don't know," Dr. Farah said. "Perhaps it's outside."

"Maybe," Amal said. "Do you think there's construction going on tonight?"

Dr. Farah shook his head. "Who would be working now at this hour?"

Amal nearly laughed. "Dad," she said, "*you're* working at this hour."

Her father chuckled and wrapped an arm around his daughter's shoulders. "Well, I think it's time I call it a night. Let's get some dinner."

"*Finally*," Amal said. "I'm *starving*."

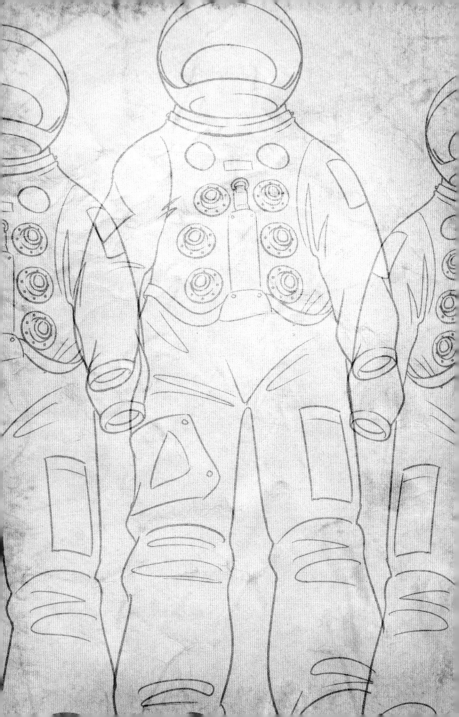

## CHAPTER 2
## Something Spooky

"I'm telling you, Clementine, you would have been scared out of your mind," Amal said as she sat on the floor of her bedroom with her phone tucked into her headscarf. She needed her hands because while she told her friend about the mysterious noises of the night before, she was also working on a scale model of NASA's interstellar probe *Voyager 1*.

21

*This headscarf is the best hands-free device ever,* Amal thought.

"Oh, stop," Clementine replied, bringing Amal's attention back to their conversation. "It's not like some flickering lights would have me crying."

Amal didn't reply. She just grinned. The truth was, she'd seen Clementine cry for less. "The point is," Amal said, "there's a mystery at the museum, and we have to solve it."

"I don't see why it's our problem," Clementine said. "Let the security guards figure it out. If it's even a mystery. It was probably just some normal museum work. It's not like you've ever been in the museum that late before."

"Well, no," Amal admitted. "I haven't. But my dad thought it was weird too."

Amal listened to Clementine sigh and moan. "What's wrong?" she asked.

"I'm working on a painting right now," Clementine replied, sounding distracted.

Amal smiled to herself. That explained it. Clementine was art-obsessed, and when she had a new project on her mind it was hard for her to think about anything else.

"What are you painting?" Amal asked.

Clementine sighed once more. "A space-scape," she said.

"Ooh," Amal said. "That sounds amazing."

As if a switch had been flipped, Clementine's mood brightened. "I knew you'd like it," she said. "I've been wanting to show it to you. I just love it. And not just because it's been fun to paint. Think about the words *space* and *scape*. They're almost the same word!"

Amal had never thought of that before. In fact, she'd never thought of a space-scape before at all. "Since when are you into painting space?" she asked. "I thought you usually only painted boring things like houses and railroad tracks and old silos — or just crazy colors that don't look like anything."

"I've been hanging out with you too much," Clementine said. Amal could hear the smile in her voice. "Just give me a few hours. I'll meet you at the museum after lunch, okay?"

"Great," Amal said. "See you then."
Now she just had to hope they'd hear those noises again.

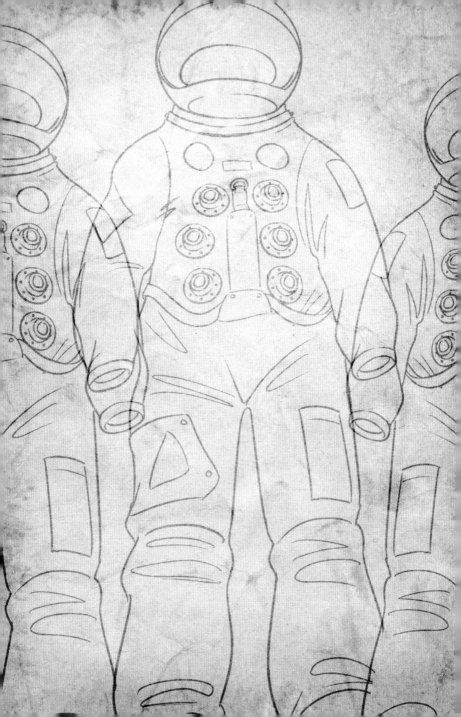

## CHAPTER 3
## Stolen!

"It was definitely coming from here?" Clementine asked later that afternoon. She and Amal stood facing the blank concrete wall at the back of the Air and Space Museum.

"Definitely," Amal said, nodding. She patted the wall with her hand twice. "I'm sure of it."

"Maybe you heard . . . I don't know," Clementine said with a shrug. "An echo?"

Amal frowned. She didn't want to admit it, but that made sense. After all, this was a concrete hallway that looped back on both ends toward the rest of the museum.

"Or maybe someone was working on a new exhibit or something," Clementine suggested as she walked the length of the concrete wall, running her hand across the surface as she went. "I mean, back in the main part of the museum. Maybe it just *sounded* like the sound was coming from here."

Amal bit the inside of her cheek. It sounded reasonable, but she was so sure . . .

*Shh . . . clomp!*

"What's that?" Amal asked, grabbing her friend's wrist. "Listen."

*Shh . . . clomp!*

The strange sound grew louder, but it wasn't coming from the other side of the wall.

Clementine huddled closer and then shook her head. "See? It must have been the echo you heard."

The *shuffle-clomp, shuffle-clomp* grew louder and louder. It echoed off the concrete wall behind Amal and Clementine and rang in their ears. The girls crouched together, the wall at their backs, and kept their eyes on the corner, waiting for some horrible monster to appear.

First came its shadow, bent and shuffling along. The creature wielded a huge ax, which it pushed along the ground in front of it.

*Shh . . . clomp! Shh . . . clomp!*

And then, with a great bellowing cough, it appeared.

"Ms. Bocharova!" Amal shouted.

Rather than a monster with an ax, it was an old woman and her wide-head push broom. The broom went *shhh . . .* as she pushed it and *clomp* when she picked it up and dropped it down again.

"Hello, child," the old custodian said. "Vhat are you doing so deep in the bowels of the museum?" Though she'd been working at the museum for twenty years, Ms. Bocharova still spoke with a very thick Russian accent. Amal sometimes heard the woman mutter to herself in Russian as she worked.

"Oh, just wandering," Amal said as she looped her arm into Clementine's elbow. "Showing my friend around."

"That's nice," Ms. Bocharova said as she pushed the broom onward down the hall. Halfway down the corridor, she began singing a boisterous song in Russian. Her voice faded as she moved around the corner.

"She's so weird," Amal said as they headed down the hall in the opposite direction.

"Oh, I think she's lovely," Clementine said. "I need something to go in the foreground of my space-scape, and I'd love to paint her."

"Ms. Bocharova, like, on another planet?" Amal said, aghast. "Clementine, how would she *breathe*?"

"Oh, good point," Clementine said. "Oh, well."

The girls spent the rest of the afternoon wandering through their favorite exhibits. Clementine occasionally commented on something that she thought would make a good addition to her space-scape.

"This might work," she said as they moved slowly through the simulated moon landing. She nodded toward the hulking metal contraption at the back of the exhibit.

The girls made their way over to the display. Walking through the exhibit was like a dream. The ground was extra bouncy to remind visitors of the low gravity on the moon, and the lighting was eerie and dim.

"This is the first lunar module," Amal said as they reached the spacecraft and stepped up to peer inside. The interior was all buttons and levers and cold-looking gray metal. There were two little triangular windows at the front. "From the *Apollo 11* mission. I mean, it's a copy of it."

"Oh, that's a shame," Clementine said. "If I were flying through space and landing on the moon, I'd want *huge* windows." She opened up her arms as wide as she could. "And I'd want my easel and paints. Which reminds me, I definitely think I should add this to my space-scape later."

Amal rolled her eyes. "If you're not painting the moon, painting a lunar module doesn't really make sense."

Clementine just shrugged. "Oh, well."

The girls bounced on into the Space Missions Timeline exhibit. There they found something very familiar.

"Wilson! Raining!" Amal exclaimed, catching sight of their two closest friends and frequent mystery-solving partners at the far end of the timeline.

"What are you two doing here?" Clementine called to them.

"We've been all over the museum," Wilson said. "Looking for you."

"Right," Raining said, a little out of breath. "There's been a robbery at my dad's museum. A space suit has been stolen!"

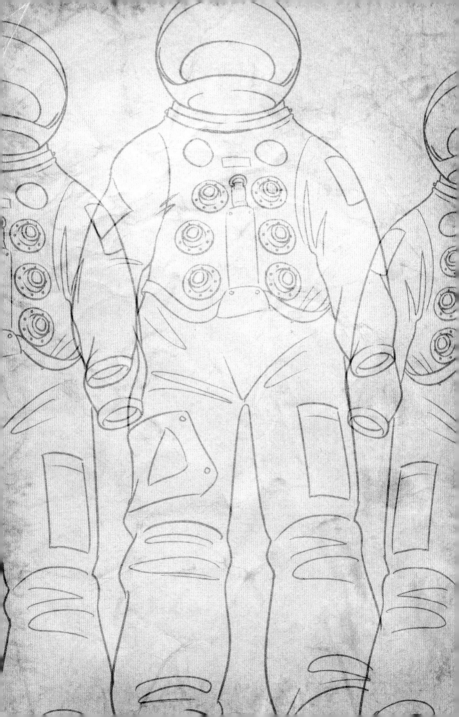

CHAPTER 4

A Mystery Afoot

"A space suit?" Amal said. "Why would there be a space suit at the American History Museum instead of here?"

"It's part of a special exhibit," Raining explained. His father, Mr. Aarik Sam, was the head of education programs at the museum, so it wasn't actually *his* museum, but he worked there. "It's only there for a couple of months, part of the Famous Astronauts of the Twentieth Century exhibit."

As Raining explained, the four friends moved toward the middle of the Space Mission Timeline.

"Ooh, I want to see it," Clementine said. "Why haven't we seen it?"

"Because it hasn't even opened yet," Raining said, taking a seat on the gleaming steel bench near the center of the room. The bench faced the museum's own collection of space suits. "It was supposed to open this weekend, but I don't know what they'll do now."

"What was so special about the space suit?" Amal asked, confused. After all, the Air and Space Museum had lots of space suits in their collection. Why would a thief decide to grab one from the American History Museum?

"It was Sally Ride's," Raining said. "She was —"

"One of the first women in space!" Amal interrupted. "After Valentina Tereshkova, I mean. I can't believe her space suit is going to be on display at *your* museum next week and you didn't tell me? How could you not tell me?"

"Take it easy!" Raining said, edging away from her to hide behind Wilson. "I was going to tell you. But it's *not* going to be on display next week, remember? It got stolen."

Amal took a deep breath and straightened herself. "Okay," she said. "We'll have to get it back."

Clementine wrapped an arm around her friend's shoulder. "I know you're upset," she said, "but don't you think a theft like this is sort of out of our league?"

"Yeah," Wilson agreed. "We should let the police handle this. It's a big deal. It'll be all over the national news, I bet."

"But isn't it weird?" Amal said, staring at the Air and Space Museum's collection of suits. "I mean, look around — Buzz Aldrin, Neil Armstrong, Alan Bean, Frank Borman, Charles Duke . . . it goes on and on. We have almost twenty space suits here. Why take that one?"

Amal looked at her friends, but they seemed as stumped as she was.

"Maybe it was easier to get at," Raining suggested. "It wasn't on the floor and on display yet."

"Maybe," Wilson said. "But Amal is right. It *is* strange."

"Then it's settled," Amal said, grinning. "We go to Raining's museum, pronto, and investigate."

"But what about your weird sounds?" Clementine asked. "Don't we already have a mystery to solve *here*?"

Amal ignored Raining's and Wilson's confused looks. "Forget about that," she said. "It sounds like the *real* mystery is going on over there."

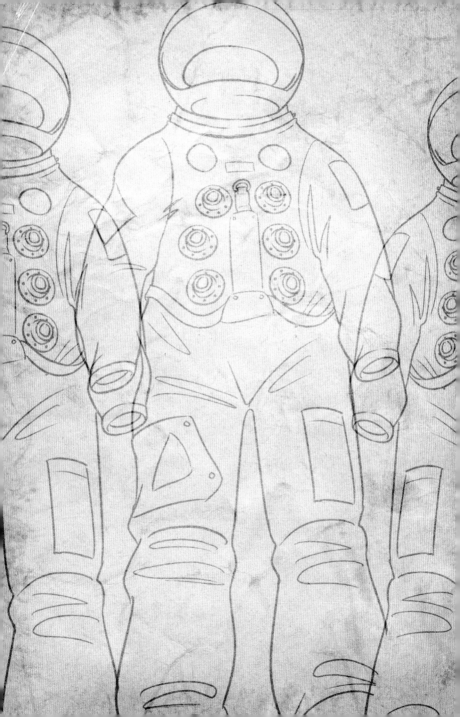

## CHAPTER 5
## Very Special Souvenir

"I told you," Wilson whispered to Amal later that afternoon. "We should leave it up to the police."

"Bah!" said Amal, but she knew Wilson was right. The touring-exhibit hall, where the American History Museum's Famous Astronauts display sat unfinished, was blocked off by three police officers and strips of yellow crime-scene tape.

Just outside the blocked-off area stood a police detective talking on her cell phone.

Reporters from the local TV stations crowded the officer and shouted questions at her:

"How did the thief have access?"

"What was stolen from the touring exhibit?"

"Will this mean the end of the Famous Astronauts tour?"

Wilson shot his friends a glance. "Boy, these reporters know less about the case than we do," he said quietly.

"Well," Raining said as his father stepped through the archway, "we do have an informant on the inside."

Mr. Sam strode over to the police detective, who'd managed to escape from the crowd of reporters. "Detective!" he called out. "It's urgent that I speak with you."

The detective, a tall woman with brown hair and a nose like a hawk's beak, hung up her phone call and peered at Mr. Sam. "Yes?" she said. "And you are . . . ?"

"My name is Aarik Sam," he said. "I work here at the museum, and I have some information you might be able to use."

"I'm Detective Archer," the woman said, pulling a little notebook and pencil from the pocket of her blazer. "Please go on. Anything might help."

Mr. Sam nodded. "As you probably know," he began, "Capitol City has a renowned air and space museum. A member of their staff — Mr. Mordecai, the director of their special collections division — has been up in arms about our hosting of this exhibit."

"Why?" the detective asked.

"Because of the very item that has been stolen," Mr. Sam explained. "He just doesn't understand why such an important artifact — the space suit worn by Sally Ride — should be housed here, rather than at his museum."

"Isn't it part of the tour?" the detective asked. "Shouldn't it stay *with* the tour?"

Mr. Sam nodded vigorously. "That's exactly what I've been telling him for the past three months," he said. "But he won't accept it!"

The detective jotted some notes on her pad, then closed it up and slipped it back into her pocket. "Thank you," she said. "If you think of anything else that might seem important, let me know." With that, she turned away, took her phone out again, and started dialing.

Amal pulled her friends to the side. "I think your dad is on to something, Raining," she whispered.

"He is?" Raining said. "How do you know?"

"Because *my* dad was at work late last night dealing with Mr. Mordecai," Amal explained. "He said he's been 'just furious' about something, but he didn't say what. He must have meant the Sally Ride space suit."

"Then we have our first suspect," said Wilson. He pulled his tablet from his backpack and entered the name *Mordecai.* "Can we speak to him?"

"We can try," Amal said. "I hope he's not as grumpy as my dad said."

Clementine nodded, wide-eyed. "I much prefer talking to people who are smiling," she said.

The four friends walked away from the crime scene and back through the main lobby toward the ticket desk. On the way, they passed a group of women and girls, all wearing matching red, white, and blue Sally Ride T-shirts. Most of them looked pretty upset.

"I guess they heard their hero's space suit isn't here anymore," Amal said.

"If they're such big fans," Raining said, "maybe one of them wanted a very special souvenir."

"Hmm," Wilson said thoughtfully. "That's a possibility. But where would they have stashed it?"

Raining stepped up to the ticket counter. "Hi, Katie."

"Afternoon, Raining," Katie, the ticket seller, replied. "Too bad about the touring exhibit, huh?"

Raining nodded. "Do you know anything about that group?" he asked. "The ones in the T-shirts?"

"Oh, sure," Katie replied. "They got the group rate. They all came together on that big charter bus parked outside."

Raining and the others glanced over at the huge glass front door and saw a gleaming silver bus parked in the lot. It was so big it took up five whole parking spaces at the back of the lot.

"What do you think?" Raining asked. "Could it be stashed out there?"

The friends made their way over to the door and stood at the glass, looking out. Their breath fogged up the window.

"Wait," Clementine said. "You don't think one of them . . . but they seem so sad!"

"Maybe one of them is a great actor," Wilson said.

"And maybe," Amal added, "Raining is right and whoever took the space suit stowed it on that bus."

Clementine twisted her mouth. "I don't know . . ."

"We should check," Raining said. He pushed open the door and walked outside. Amal and Wilson joined him, and a moment later Clementine hurried after.

"But what about Mr. Mordecai and the Air and Space Museum?" Clementine asked as she caught up to the others.

"We'll head over there next," Amal said. "Don't worry."

## CHAPTER 6
## Bus–ted

Amal strode right up to the bus's door and knocked three times on the shiny silver.

Nothing happened.

She knocked again — louder this time — and behind the black tint of the window she saw movement. A moment later, a gruff-looking face peered through.

"Who are you?" the figure snapped. His voice was muffled by the closed door.

"Can you open the door?" Amal shouted. "We can't hear you!"

"What?!" the man shouted back.

"Open the door!" the kids shouted together.

The gruff face disappeared from the window.

"I guess he's not going to open the door," Clementine muttered. She put her face up to the window and tried to peer inside.

But a moment later, there was a thud and a hiss. Clementine jumped back, and the door opened. It reminded Amal of a spaceship door from a science fiction movie. Except there was no alien behind this door — just a very annoyed bus driver.

"Well?" the man snapped. "What do you want?"

"Umm . . . ," said Clementine. She shuffled backward and ducked behind her friends. "Nothing."

"Actually," said Wilson, "we want to look for something on your bus."

The bus driver sneered and scratched at the stubble on his chin. "Look for what?"

"A space suit," Raining said.

"A *what*?" the driver said.

Amal elbowed Raining and laughed. "He's kidding," she said. "Actually, um, my grandmother is on the tour, and she left her pills on the bus. I need to get them for her before she starts feeling sick."

"Your grandmother's on the tour," the driver said, sounding doubtful.

Amal nodded.

"But you're not," he said. He raised an eyebrow.

"Right," said Amal, nodding again.

"You live in Capitol City," the driver said.

"Yep," Amal said.

The driver reached into his pocket and pulled out a toothpick. He bared his teeth and picked at the narrow gap between his front bottom teeth. "There's a woman on the tour who could be your grandmother, I suppose," he said after a moment. "She's in seat 8A."

He stepped back onto the bus and sat in the driver's seat. There, he grabbed a magazine from the huge dashboard and flipped it open. "Help yourself."

Amal quickly climbed aboard. "Thank you."

The others started to follow her, but the driver coughed and said, "Ah, ah! Not so fast. Just the girl with the sick grandma. You three wait outside."

Wide-eyed, Amal looked back at the others, but they only shrugged up at her. She'd have to do this on her own. The door closed behind her.

The bus was long and dark. It smelled musty, like old socks and wet paper bags, but also like chemical cleansers and motor oil. Amal walked toward the back, counting as she went, until she got to row eight. Then she knelt down on the carpet floor and looked under the seat.

Nothing. Not even a bag lunch or a purse or a dropped nickel.

Next she stood on the edge of the seat to reach the overheard luggage compartments, but that was empty too. No space suit. No helmet.

"She could have put it anywhere," Amal whispered to herself. "I have to check the other seats too." She started walking deeper into the bus, scanning the seats and under the seats as she went.

"Hey!" the bus driver suddenly shouted. Amal spun and saw him watching her in the rearview mirror. "I said seat 8A. Where are you going?"

"Oh," Amal said, forcing a smile. "I couldn't find the pills. I thought maybe the bottle rolled to the back."

The driver seemed to growl like an impatient pit bull. "Fine," he said. "You've got sixty seconds."

"Why?" Amal asked. "Are you leaving?"

"I'm not going anywhere until the tour leaves town at eight tonight," the driver replied shortly. "I just want you off my bus!"

Amal quickly knelt down and crawled the rest of the way to the back. She wanted to climb up on the seats and check every overhead compartment too, but the driver wouldn't have let her. Besides, she didn't have much time.

By the time Amal reached the very back of the bus and climbed to her feet, her time was up. The driver stood up and opened the door.

"Okay, kid," he said. He pulled the toothpick from his mouth and used it to point out the door. "Time's up. Out you go."

"But I haven't found the pills yet," Amal protested.

"Sorry," the driver said. "And sorry to grandma too. But you're out of time."

"Okay," Amal said. She kept her eyes on the floor as she walked back up the aisle. When she reached the steps, she stopped and turned around. "Hey, maybe she left it in the big storage compartment under the bus. Do you think you could unlock it for —"

"Get outta here!" the driver snarled at her.

The instant Amal's foot hit the parking lot blacktop, the door *whooshed* closed again.

"No luck, huh?" Raining said.

Amal shook her head. "He's mean."

"Maybe he's involved," Wilson said as they started walking back toward the museum. "Maybe he didn't want you poking around too much because he was afraid you'd find something."

Amal shook her head. "I doubt it. I think sometimes people are just big meanies," she said. "What time is it?"

Wilson checked his watch — he was the only one of them who wore one. "Almost five."

"Oh, no!" Amal said. "The Air and Space closes at five! And we haven't questioned Mr. Mordecai yet."

"We'd better hurry," Raining said. "We can cut across the Big Lawn." He nodded in the direction of the big expanse of grass that sat between the four major Capitol City museums. The museums sometimes used it for special outdoor events. It was also a great place for kite flying, Frisbee throwing, or just lying in the sunshine.

"We'll never make it in time," Amal said as they hurried around the side of the American History Museum. "But it's Saturday. I have a plan. Does everyone have some money?"

## CHAPTER 7
## In Need of a Suspect

Thirty minutes later, Amal led them
to the side entrance of the Air and
Space Museum. Luckily for them, the
planetarium had special after-hours shows
right up till midnight on Saturday nights.
They had to buy four tickets — to the
five-thirty showing of "Are Black Holes
Doorways . . . or Death Traps?" — but they
got in.

"Okay," Amal said over her shoulder to her friends. "Let's find Mr. Mordecai. I think I know where his office is. Hopefully he's working a little late."

She shoved the tickets into her back pocket and, rather than following the line of planetarium visitors, moved toward the archway into the rest of the museum. But she didn't make it to the archway. She hadn't been watching where she was going, and she walked right into the powerful midsection of Margaret Heckles, night security guard.

"Ms. Farah," the big woman said. "Did you forget how to get inside the planetarium?"

"Oh!" Amal said. "Hi, Maggie. Didn't see you there."

The security guard leaned down and snarled at her. "My name is *Margaret*," she said through her teeth. "I don't even let my *mother* call me Maggie. Got it?"

"Sorry," Amal said. She actually knew that. Margaret had given her the same instructions at least five times. "Won't happen again."

"See that it doesn't," said the security guard. "Now get back in the planetarium line before I escort you and your three troublemaker friends right out of the museum."

The four kids jumped and hurried to the back of the line.

"Now what do we do?" Clementine whispered.

Amal shrugged. "I guess we learn all about black holes."

* * *

"That was marvelous," Clementine said as she, Amal, Wilson, and Raining stepped out of the planetarium theater. Though the others were bleary-eyed and woozy, Clementine was more animated than she'd been all day. "Breathtaking! Inspiring!"

"Nauseating," Raining said, holding his belly.

"Nonsense," Clementine said. "I feel so close to a true breakthrough in my space-scape painting. That was just what I needed."

The exiting crowd headed for the doors, but Amal stopped and looked around.

"Okay," she said quietly. "I don't see Maggie anywhere. Let's move fast."

"Mr. Mordecai probably isn't even here anymore," Clementine said. "It's after six-thirty."

"Yeah, Amal," Wilson said. "Forget it. He probably went home to have dinner."

"Which is what I'd like to do now," Raining said. "It's taco night."

"Not yet," Amal said, pleading with her friends. "Even if Mr. Mordecai is already gone, this would be a great time to check for the mysterious noises."

"What noises?" Wilson asked.

Amal told Wilson and Raining all about the weird noises she and her father had heard the night before — the noises she'd thought were the big mystery until the space suit went missing.

"So why now?" Wilson said.

"Because it was after hours last time," Amal explained. "Come on. Hurry, before Maggie shows up again."

The group followed Amal through the darkened exhibits and high-ceilinged corridors of the museum until they reached the MUSEUM EMPLOYEES ONLY door. Ignoring the sign, Amal swung it open, ushered the others inside, and let it close behind them.

The back halls were as dark as the front of the museum, lit only by the eerie red light of the exit signs at every intersection. Light also leaked out from beneath one office door, which bore a black placard that read *Mortimer Mordecai, Head of Special Collections.*

Amal put out her arms to stop the others. "Look," she whispered. "The lights are on. Do you think he's still here?"

"Let's find out," Raining said. He slipped past Amal and knocked twice on the door.

An instant later the door opened just a crack, and Mr. Mordecai's face appeared. He wasn't much taller than Clementine, but his face and attitude weren't nearly as pleasant.

"Who is it?" Mr. Mordecai said. His voice was shrill and breathy, like an angry snake might sound if angry snakes could talk. "That annoying detective has been hounding me all day, and now this. What do you want?"

"Mr. Mordecai," Amal said, stepping toward the door. "You know my father, right?"

"Yes, yes," he said, clearly exasperated. "Dr. Farah. He's a thorn in my side. Are you trying out to be another thorn too?"

Amal stared at the man. "What?" she said.

"Oh, just tell me what you *want,* child!" he snapped.

"Um . . . ," Amal started to say, but she was too upset by Mr. Mordecai's nasty words about her father to continue.

Clementine took over. "Have you heard about the missing space suit?" she asked.

"Yes, of course," said Mr. Mordecai, and for a moment a look of pure glee flashed across his face. "Leave it to *that* museum

to lose something so precious so quickly."
His expression quickly soured again. "For
some reason that detective thinks *I* had
something to do with it. But I haven't been
to that museum in *years*."

Mr. Mordecia fired a withering glance
at Amal. "Tell your father it's his fault, will
you?" he snapped. "If I'd had *my* way, the
space suit would be safe and sound right
here, which is where it should have been
the whole time!"

With that, he slammed the door in their
faces.

"Wow," Clementine said. "That
completely killed the inspiration buzz I got
from the planetarium show."

"We are just meeting the meanest
people today," Wilson said.

Amal nodded. "Let's go," she said. Mr. Mordecai's words stung, and after the run-in with Maggie and the mean bus driver, she'd had enough for one day. "Let's forget the whole thing. Raining, maybe you can still make it home for taco night."

"But what about the mystery?" Raining said. "Mr. Mordecai has already spoken to the detective, and it sounds like he didn't do it."

"Yeah," agreed Wilson. "We need a new suspect."

"Who cares?" Amal snapped. "Let the police worry about it. I'm going home." And she headed for the exit.

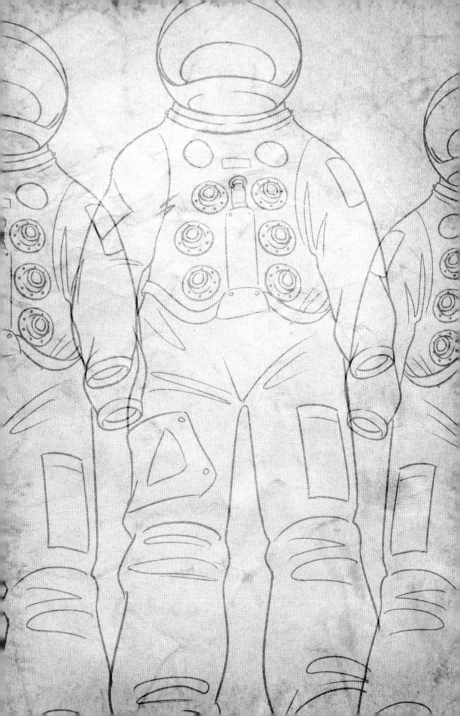

## CHAPTER 8
## Unexplained Noises

"Amal, don't," Clementine said, hurrying to her friend's side. "Don't let that jerk upset you."

"Yeah," Wilson added as he joined them. "That's just what he wanted to do."

"Don't give him the satisfaction," Raining said.

Amal shrugged and leaned against the wall near the door to the main part of the museum. It had a narrow window up one side. Through it, she could just see into the Moon Walk exhibit. "It's not my dad's fault, right?" she said, taking her eyes off the window for a moment.

"Of course not," Clementine said. "It's a crummy thief's fault."

"Right," Raining agreed. "Besides, if we're going to start blaming dads, mine was more in charge of the space suit than yours was."

Amal laughed. "True!" she said. "So what do we do now?" She put her hands on the door to push it open, but as she did so, she saw something through the window that made her heart skip a beat.

"Someone's coming!" Amal hissed at the others. "Get down!"

The four kids immediately dropped to the floor and held their breath.

"Is it Maggie?" Raining asked.

"I couldn't tell!" Amal said.

From the other side of the door, slow footsteps grew louder and louder.

"Oh, no," Amal whispered. "She's coming over here."

The footsteps thumped right up to the door and stopped.

"What do we do?" Raining hissed.

"We run," Amal said. "Let's go!"

The four kids, still crouched and out of sight, took off down the hallway, right past Mr. Mordecai's office and into the labyrinth of the museum's back hallways.

"Do you even know where we are anymore?" Wilson asked Amal.

"Of course," said Amal. And she did . . . sort of. At least, she was sure she'd been in this hallway before once or twice. Maybe just once.

They'd been walking through the dark back corridors for at least fifteen minutes, every so often hurrying ahead and taking a few quick turns when they heard footsteps. Suddenly Clementine said, "I know this place."

Amal realized at once her friend was right — it was the weird dead end where she'd first heard the mysterious noises.

"I haven't heard any footsteps in a while," Wilson said. "Do you think she's gone?"

"I don't know!" said Amal.

"Shhh!" Raining said. "Someone will hear us!"

But their voices were soon drowned out by the *clanging* and *banging* and *whirring* coming from behind the cement block wall.

"That's it!" Amal said, now shouting with glee. She was sure Maggie would come around a corner any moment and catch them here, but she didn't care. She was too thrilled that her friends had finally heard the mysterious noise. "That's the noise my dad and I heard last night!"

The others listened a moment.

"Sounds like maintenance work," Raining said. He had to shout now too to be heard over the racket.

"My dad would have known about scheduled maintenance or repairs," Amal pointed out. "He was as stumped as I was."

The noises stopped abruptly, and Amal's last shouts hung in the air and echoed through the cement hall. The kids exchanged worried looks, sure that the security guard would have heard them. Sure enough, after a minute of dead silence, the footsteps returned.

"She's coming," Clementine whispered.

"We're caught for sure," Wilson said.

The footsteps moved closer and closer.

But Amal realized something wasn't quite right. Those weren't Maggie's footsteps. They shuffled. They squeaked. Those weren't the footsteps of a woman built like a tree. They were the footsteps of . . .

"Ms. Bocharova!"

Clementine and Amal said her name at the same time. It was the old Russian cleaning lady, pushing her garbage can on wheels. Her big broom stood upright inside it.

"Vhat are you kids doing back here?" Ms. Bocharova asked, her accent as thick as ever. "Don't you know museum is closed?"

"We know," Amal said. "We went to the planetarium show."

"They're open late on Saturdays," Raining pointed out.

"Vhat, you think I don't know that, smart guy?" Ms. Bocharova said. "I've seen every show, probably five times each! I know more about space and ships than anyvone on staff here!"

"Okay," Raining said.

"We got a little lost in the halls after the show, that's all," Clementine said.

"Lost," Ms. Bocharova said, smiling. "You four? Ha! You think I don't know who you kids are? You four could get around every museum in this city vith your eyes closed and one leg tied behind your back."

"Well . . ." Amal began, "you know . . . we heard all that banging and decided to come see what it was."

"Do *you* know what it was, Ms. Bocharova?" Clementine asked.

"Banging?" the old woman repeated, shaking her head. She started pushing her garbage can along once again. "I don't hear so good anymore." With that, she turned the corner and was gone.

"Boy, she is *weird*," Raining muttered.

"I like her," Clementine said.

"She could have gotten us in trouble," Wilson said. "But she didn't. That has to count for something."

"True," Raining said. "Who is she?"

Amal shrugged as she led the group back through the corridors toward the exit. "She's the janitor."

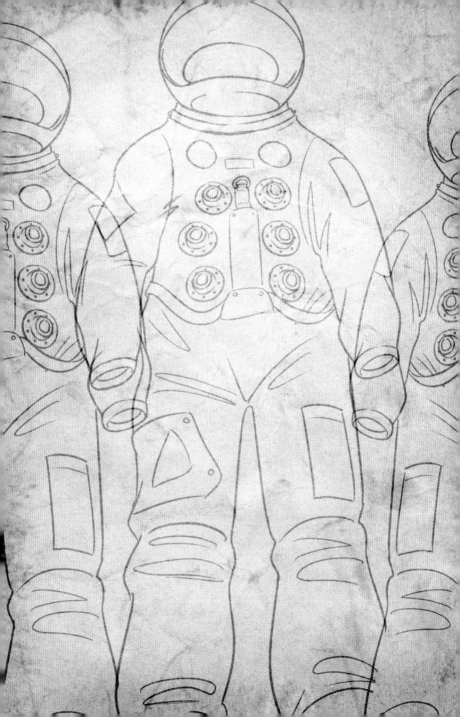

## CHAPTER 9
## What Are We Missing?

All day Sunday, Amal did her best to think about anything other than weird noises in back hallways and Sally Ride space suits. But on Monday morning, when she accompanied her father to the museum, the mysteries confronted her almost immediately.

"Oh, great," Amal muttered to herself as the morning security guard opened the side door for her and her father.

Gathered in a loud, agitated group were dozens of women in Sally Ride T-shirts.

"I guess they heard that we have a pretty decent Ride collection right here," her father said proudly as they went inside.

"I heard they were leaving on Saturday night," Amal said.

"Where'd you hear that?" her father asked.

She shrugged. "I don't remember." She couldn't tell him she interrogated the bus driver, after all.

Amal followed her dad as far as the MUSEUM EMPLOYEES ONLY door. "Dad, I'm going to call my friends," she said. "You go ahead."

"All right," said her father. "You know where to find me if you need me for anything."

"Right-o," Amal said. She waited a moment, until her dad was well behind the door, and then dialed Clementine.

"Morning!" Clementine answered cheerfully.

"You have to come down here right away," Amal said. "The Sally Ride fans are *here.*"

"Here?" Clementine repeated. "Where are you?"

"I'm at the Air and Space Museum," Amal said. "Obviously. Where are you?"

"I'm locking my bike up at school," Clementine said. "Class starts in like five minutes! Shouldn't you get down here too?"

Amal rolled her eyes. She adored Clementine. But sometimes . . .

"Is it kind of quiet down there?" Amal said.

Clementine was silent for a moment. "I guess," she said. "Oh no, am I late? Is everyone inside already?"

"Clementine," Amal said, "there's no school today. It's a holiday."

"It is?" Clementine said. "Wow, that explains why the bus never came."

Amal shook her head. "I'm going to call the others. Come down here, okay?"

Anyone else would have felt pretty silly. Maybe embarrassed. Maybe angry. But not

Clementine. Her voice was as bright as a mirror in the sunshine when she said, "I'll be right there!"

Next Amal called Raining and Wilson — they were both at home with nothing better to do — then headed to the front desk. She found Kenny, the newest member of the staff, getting ready to open the ticket counter.

"Hi, Amal," Kenny said, nearly as cheerful as Clementine. He'd only been with the museum for a short time, but Amal liked him already. He was always friendly to her, and he remembered her name right away. That almost never happened.

"Hi, Kenny," Amal said. "What's with the group at the doors waiting to get in?"

Kenny glanced at the T-shirt-clad fan club. "I guess they're a bunch of Sally Ride fans," he said. "You know who she is?"

Amal rolled her eyes. "Of course I do!"

Kenny shrugged. "I had no idea," he admitted. "But apparently we have a bunch of stuff about her here at the museum, and they're here to see it."

"I saw them at the American History Museum on Saturday," Amal said.

Kenny nodded and frowned. "Their guide told me," he said. "They had to rework the itinerary for their trip to make the time to come over here after the disappointment over there."

*That explains why they're still in town,* Amal thought. *I guess Dad was right.*

"Well, time to unlock the doors," Kenny said, rising from his stool. "See you around, Amal."

Amal nodded and leaned against the ticket counter. As Kenny unlocked the glass doors, she watched the group of Sally Ride fans outside. They were all on their toes, any depression and disappointment gone from their midst. As soon as the door was open, the Ride fans walked in, pressed together, each of them vying for the chance to be the first to reach the collection of Sally Ride artifacts.

The mob of red, white, and blue T-shirts moved through the lobby. Their guide, a tall woman wearing the same T-shirt plus a bright white baseball cap, headed through the first archway, from which visitors could go anywhere in the museum.

"This way!" the guide chirped back at the group. They trailed after her like a flock of ducklings following their mother.

"Amal!" Clementine called as she ran into the lobby. Raining and Wilson were right behind her. "Did you see who was with the group?"

Amal shook her head.

"Ms. Bocharova!" Clementine exclaimed. "The cleaning lady!"

Amal turned to look and caught a glimpse of the old Russian woman as the Ride fans disappeared through the archway. She ran after her and caught her at the next corner.

"Hello," Ms. Bocharova said. "Why do I keep running into you?"

"What are you doing with the tour?" Amal asked, ignoring Ms. Bocharova's question. "Were you at the American History Museum last week too?"

"Why shouldn't I be with the tour?" Ms. Bocharova said.

"Um, because you live in this city," Amal said. "And you work in this museum? Why would you need a tour?"

"I didn't ride the bus with them, child," Ms. Bocharova said. "But I am a member of the Sally Ride fan club. In fact, I'm the local chapter president."

"Huh," said Amal.

"You are so surprised?" Ms. Bocharova said. "Sally Ride was an inspiration for many women in the sciences, including me."

"Including you?" Amal said. "But —"

"But nothing," Ms. Bocharova cut her off. "I must go. You've made me lose the tour. I will catch up. Goodbye." She hurried off down the wide, white corridor toward the History of NASA exhibit, leaving Amal alone in the hall.

Her friends joined her a moment later.

"I don't get it," Amal said after she'd told the others everything the Russian woman had said. "She said 'women in the sciences.' But she's a janitor at a museum. That doesn't count as 'in the sciences.' What are we missing?"

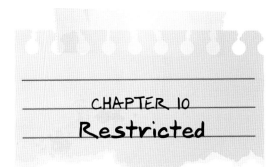

## CHAPTER 10
## Restricted

After checking the back hallway for noise and hearing nothing unusual, the kids headed outside to the Big Lawn. It was a beautiful day, and it seemed like a good place to have lunch and stare at the sky, waiting for inspiration — at least that's what Clementine thought.

"So many terrific clouds today," she said, lying on her back and staring up at the sky and the back of the Air and Space Museum. It was all concrete and glass, very sleek and modern, and built into the side of the hill.

"That one looks like a sleeping lion," Clementine continued, not bothering to point. "And that one looks like a steamship."

"I don't see it," said Wilson, who was lying next to her. He usually didn't see it.

"Oh! And there's a cup of tea!" Clementine exclaimed. "It's even steaming."

"What?" Wilson said, staring straight up. "I don't see that."

"You're looking the wrong way, silly," Clementine said. She was up on her elbows looking at the back of the museum.

Then Wilson saw it too — twenty yards or so from the back of the museum, near the edge of the winding path that crossed the Big Lawn and connected the four museums, billowed a column of thick steam. It looked like a cloud coming right out of the ground.

Wilson hopped up and ran to it. It came from the vent next to the path. "Amal!" he shouted. She and Raining were throwing a foam football back and forth close-by. "What is this?"

Amal glanced over. "I don't know," she said. "A steam vent?"

"But from where?" Wilson asked as Raining joined him beside the vent. "The museum doesn't have a basement, does it?"

Amal shook her head and joined the boys at the steam column. "No," she said, "but it's set into the hill. This would be the very back of the first floor."

"In other words," Clementine said, getting to her feet and grinning, "it would be just about where the noise is coming from."

Amal's mouth dropped open. The foam football dropped to the grass. She ran to

Clementine and threw her arms around her. "You're right!" she said. "Wherever this steam is coming from is where the noise is coming from!"

"How did you figure that out so quickly?" Wilson said.

Clementine wrinkled her nose at him. "It's obvious," she said. "You just don't have a good sense of space. I get it from painting and sculpting and drawing."

Raining, meanwhile, had wandered off along the winding path. He'd found other vents, some with steam and some without. Suddenly he spotted something he'd seen a hundred times or more but never really thought about. "Guys!" he called across the Big Lawn. "What's in there?"

Amal looked over. Raining pointed down at a big metal garage door painted in yellow-

and-black stripes and built right into the side of the hill itself.

Together, the four kids ran down to the check the door. A sign across the top said RESTRICTED — NO ENTRY WITHOUT AUTHORIZATION. Next to the door was a key card reader — which all the museums used for offices and restricted areas.

Amal read the sign next to the reader out loud: *"Level Double-A Security Clearance Required.* Whoa."

LEVEL
DOUBLE-A
SECURITY
CLEARANCE
REQUIRED.

"Whoa what?" Clementine asked.

"That's some serious security clearance," Amal said. "My dad doesn't even have that."

"Mine either," said Raining.

"Neither does my mom," Wilson said, shaking his head.

"So who does?" Clementine asked.

Amal shrugged. "The president, maybe?" She pulled out her phone and dialed. "Dad? It's me. Hey, what's in the weird garage built into the hill under the Big Lawn? Uh-huh . . . no reason . . . okay, thanks, Dad. See you later."

"Well?" Raining said.

"He said it's really special stuff for all the museums," Amal said. "Real ship parts, working rockets, shipments of fossils before they reach the Natural History Museum . . . that kind of stuff. But he's never been in there. Apparently only the delivery people and major big shots, like people from NASA, ever go in."

"Then it's someone from NASA banging down there?" Wilson said. "I wonder what they could be doing."

Amal frowned. She was starting to think the noises behind the wall weren't a mystery at all.

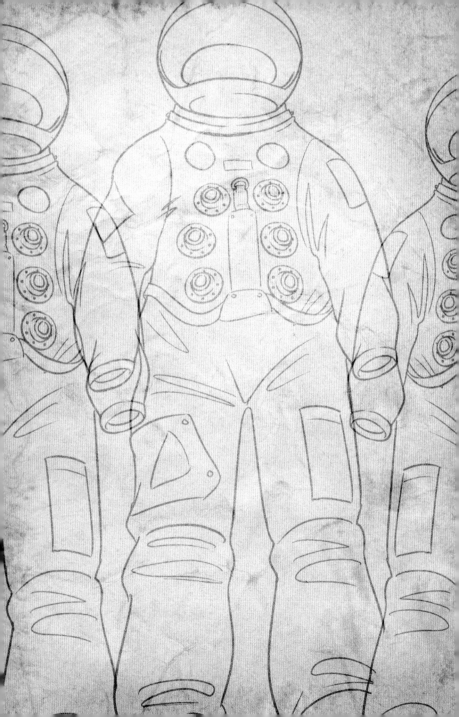

CHAPTER 11
Sally's Biggest Fan

"I have to go home," Raining said at about five that afternoon.

"Me too," said Wilson. "School tomorrow."

"Oh, right," Clementine said. "I should write that down."

Amal sighed. The four of them lay on the soft, bouncy ground of the moon room. The Sally Ride fans had long since left, their bus gone from the parking lot.

"I hope the space suit wasn't on that bus," Raining said as he stood up.

The others stood too, and together they headed for the front exit, passing through the space suit collection as they went. Wilson stopped in front of the suits one more time.

"It had to be one of them," he said. "I mean, all these suits. Whoever took it *had* to be a Sally Ride fanatic, right?"

"Why else would they *not* take one of these?" Wilson said.

Amal stepped up to the collection and read the placards one more time. "Buzz

Aldrin, Neil Armstrong, Alan Bean, Frank Borman . . . ," she said. Suddenly she stopped and grabbed Clementine's wrist.

"Ow!" Clementine exclaimed. "What?"

"Sorry," Amal said, bouncing on her toes. "Clementine, is there anything *odd* about this collection?"

"Sure," Clementine said, lifting one shoulder like it was no big thing. "There are no women in it."

"Exactly," Amal said. "Not a single *woman's* space suit in the whole collection."

"Well," Raining said, "there haven't been too many female astronauts, I guess."

"There have been lots, actually," Wilson said. He held up his tablet computer and pointed to a list of names. "See?"

"Let me see that," Amal said, grabbing the tablet.

Clementine looked over her shoulder. "The collection here needs updating," she said, squinting at the list.

"I agree," said a voice — a very distinct voice.

The four kids spun, and through the nearest archway, out of the darkness, appeared a familiar figure — Ms. Bocharova. "Such a shame that Ms. Ride's space suit should be the first woman's space suit to ever travel through our city," she said.

"You should talk to my dad about it," Amal said. "He'd probably listen to you."

"A good idea!" Ms. Bocharova said. She didn't have her rolling garbage can with her. In fact she was still in her Sally Ride T-shirt. "The museum is closing in a moment, though, so you kids better find the exit now."

"What about you?" Clementine said. "Don't you have to leave too?"

Ms. Bocharova laughed. "Of course not," she said. "I will start work in twenty minutes. Why bother leaving?"

Amal stepped up to her. "I guess you can be here pretty much whenever you please, huh?"

"What do you mean?" Ms. Bocharova asked.

"You have a key card, right?" Amal said.

The old woman pulled a card on a retractable leash from her belt and held it up. It showed her grim face and her last name. "Of course I do," she said. "How else can I get into all the rooms to clean up? Very important."

"*How* important?" Amal said. "Double-A important?"

Ms. Bocharova laughed and let the key card snap back into place. "Oh, I don't know," she said, sounding a bit nervous. "Who pays attention to that stuff? You kids better get moving before they lock the front doors."

"Ms. Bocharova," Amal pressed. "How long has it been since you went . . . up there?" She looked up at the ceiling.

"To the second floor?" Clementine said. "What does that matter?"

Ms. Bocharova laughed and sat down on the metal bench in front of the space suit collection. "No, child," she said. "Not the second floor — *space.*"

"You've been to space?" said Clementine, Wilson, and Raining all at once. Amal wasn't surprised at all, though.

Ms. Bocharova shook her head. "Not quite, but I was close. The Soviet Union once had a space program to rival that of the United States," she said. "I was one of the first women to train to go into space — before Sally Ride, even." She turned to Amal. "How did you figure it out? No one here has ever known about my past."

"First I realized that the thief might have taken the suit not just because she was a Sally Ride *fan*," Amal said, sitting beside her, "but also because it was the only one that would *fit* her properly."

Ms. Bocharova nodded. "You're right," she said. "But I am also a great fan of Sally Ride, of course."

"But I still didn't put it together until Wilson showed me that list of female astronauts and cosmonauts," Amal continued. "I saw your name."

"Oh, my," Ms. Bocharova said. "That vould give it away, vouldn't it?"

"The only thing I don't get," Amal said, "is how you got the space suit out of the history museum and into the underground garage."

"The garage connects to all the museums," Ms. Bocharova said, "if you know vhich door to use — and you have Double-A clearance."

"A collection of secret doors and tunnels connecting all the museums underground," Wilson said. "That must come in handy."

"I still don't get it," Clementine said. "What difference does it make if it's a woman's space suit? It's not like you're going up there *now*, right?"

Ms. Bocharova sighed. "Probably not," she admitted. "My time has past."

"Then why? And what are you doing back there with all the clanging and banging?" Raining asked. "Are you building something?"

Ms. Bocharova sighed. "I like you kids very much," she said. "But you are too smart for your own good. I vanted the space suit for myself. No one appreciates the contributions female astronauts have made — but I do. I planned to add the space suit to my own collection. I vas building a shipping container vith a false bottom to smuggle it out."

Amal shook her head. "That's not fair," she said. "There *are* people who appreciate the contributions female astronauts have made — people like me. And if you take that space suit, you're stealing that history from all of us."

Ms. Bocharova looked ashamed. "You're right," she admitted. "I did not think of it like that." With a groan, she rose to her feet. "I suppose I'd better get the space suit back to its rightful place. Perhaps, if I do, you vill take pity on an old woman vith big dreams and not turn me in." She gave them a hopeful look.

Amal and her friends all looked at each other. After a moment, they all nodded. "I think that's fair," Amal agreed. "But it has to go back tonight."

"Not yet!" Clementine exclaimed, thrusting her finger into the air. "First you have to try on the suit."

"Vhatever for?" Ms. Bocharova said, surprised.

"So I can take a photo of you with my phone," Clementine said. "I finally know just what to put in the foreground of my space-scape!"

**Steve B.**

## About the Author

Steve Brezenoff is the author of more than fifty middle-grade chapter books, including the Field Trip Mysteries series, the Ravens Pass series of thrillers, and the Return to Titanic series. In his spare time, he enjoys video games, cycling, and cooking. Steve lives in Minneapolis with his wife, Beth, and their son and daughter.

**Lisa W.**

## About the Illustrator

Lisa K. Weber is an illustrator currently living in Oakland, California. She graduated from Parsons School of Design in 2000 and then began freelancing. Since then, she has completed many print, animation, and design projects, including graphic novelizations of classic literature, character and background designs for children's cartoons, and textiles for dog clothing.

# $\left( \text{GLOSSARY} \right)$

**artifact** (ART-uh-fakt) — an object made by human beings, especially a tool or weapon used in the past

**boisterous** (BOI-stur-uhss) — behaving in a wild and noisy way

**evidence** (EV-uh-duhnss) — information and facts that help prove something or make you believe something is true

**exhibit** (eg-ZIB-it) — a public display of works of art, historical objects, etc.

**foreground** (FOR-ground) — the part of a picture nearest to the person looking at it

**frequent** (FREE-kwent) — happening often

**lunar** (LOO-nur) — having to do with the moon

**module** (MOJ-ool) — a separate, independent section that can be linked to other parts to make something larger

**planetarium** (pla-uh-TAIR-ee-uhm) — a building with equipment for reproducing the positions and movements of the sun, moon, planets, and stars, by projecting their images onto a curved ceiling

**rival** (RYE-vuhl) — to be as good as something or someone else

**space suit** (SPAYSS-soot) — the protective clothing that an astronaut wears in space

# DISCUSSION QUESTIONS

**1.** Who else did you think might be a suspect in this case? Talk about some possibilities and discuss why you thought that person was guilty.

**2.** Ms. Bocharova knew going back into space was unlikely, but she dreamed of doing so. Would you want to travel into outer space? Talk about why or why not.

**3.** Because her father works at the Air and Space Museum, Amal and her friends have access to exhibits and areas that would otherwise be off-limits. If you could choose a museum to have access to, which one would it be? Talk about your choice and your reasoning.

# WRITING PROMPTS

**1.** Write a chapter that continues this book. What happens after the kids solve the mystery of the stolen space suit?

**2.** There are several museums in the Capitol City network. Write a paragraph about which one you think would be most interesting to visit and why.

**3.** Amal and her friends each have their own interests and hobbies. Write a paragraph about one of your hobbies or interests. What do you enjoy about it?

# THE SPACE RACE

After the end of World War II (1939–1945), a new competition took shape — the Space Race. This 20th-century battle pitted rival nations the United States and the Soviet Union against each other. Both countries were determined to prove they had the best space technology, as well as the best scientific and economic systems.

## Space Race Timeline:

**1955** — The United States and the Soviet Union both announce they will be launching satellites into orbit.

**October 4, 1957** — The Soviet Union launches the first successful satellite, *Sputnik I*, into orbit and officially takes the lead in the Space Race. *Sputnik* is Russian for "traveler."

**January 31, 1958** — Four months after the launch of *Sputnik I*, the United States successfully launches its own satellite, *Explorer I*.

**April 12, 1961** — Yuri Gagarin, a Russian astronaut, becomes the first man to orbit Earth in the spacecraft *Vostok I*. Three weeks later, the United States launches *Freedom 7*, making astronaut Alan Shepard the first American in space.

**1961** — President John F. Kennedy, sensing the United States was being embarrassed in the Space Race, announces plans to put a man on the moon before the end of the decade and launches the Apollo program.

**February 20, 1962** — Nearly a year after the *Vostok I* was launched, the United States sends John Glenn into space on *Friendship 7*, making him the first American astronaut to orbit Earth.

**July 16, 1969** — After several years of experiments, test flights, and training, *Apollo 11*, carrying U.S. astronauts Neil Armstrong, Edwin "Buzz" Aldrin, and Michael Collins, takes off for the moon. The trip takes three days, and the spacecraft lands on the moon on July 20, 1969. Neil Armstrong becomes the first man to walk on the moon, uttering the famous words: "That's one small step for man, one giant leap for mankind."

Ready for more
MYSTERY?

# MUSEUM MYSTERIES

Check out another Capitol City sleuths' adventure and help them solve crime in some of the city's most important museums!

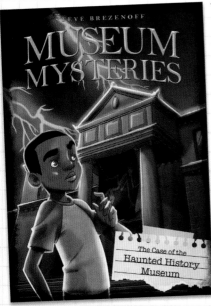

The Capitol City Natural History Museum is haunted — or at least that's what someone wants people to think. But Wilson Kipper, son of the museum's head paleontologist, knows better. When the strange occurrences start to turn dangerous, the museum is forced to close its doors. Can Wilson and his friends get to the bottom of things, or will the Natural History Museum be shut down for good?